COST OF INDEPENDENCE

10 UNFAIRY TALES

SHRIKA SOMISETTI

© **Shrika Somisetti 2023**

All rights reserved

All rights reserved by author. No part of this publication may be reproduced, stored in a retrieval system or transmitted in any form or by any means, electronic, mechanical, photocopying, recording or otherwise, without the prior permission of the author.

Although every precaution has been taken to verify the accuracy of the information contained herein, the author and publisher assume no responsibility for any errors or omissions. No liability is assumed for damages that may result from the use of information contained within.

First Published in June 2023

ISBN: 978-93-93385-25-3

BLUEROSE PUBLISHERS
www.BlueRoseONE.com
info@bluerosepublishers.com
+91 8882 898 898

Cover Design:
Muskan Sachdeva

Typographic Design:
Pooja Sharma

Distributed by: BlueRose, Amazon, Flipkart

NOTHING IS FREE OF COST-
EVEN FREEDOM.

Contents

Cost Of Independence 1

The Massacre 5

The Charge On The Crowd 12

Sacrifice, Pain And Love 16

The Terrors Of Partition 22

The Terrors Of Partition 28

The Harsh Truth 34

The Father's Wish 38

The New Girl 43

The Contradiction 46

Cost Of Independence

Young Govind walked around with a small amount of rice on his plate. He was searching for a place to eat in peace although he did not feel like doing so, not because he wasn't hungry but because of the pain and sorrow hidden inside him.

He sat under a shady tree to protect himself from the sun god's wrath on a hot summer afternoon. Looking at the small quantity of rice in his plate, he thought of his mother who would have convinced him to eat by now. Tears fell from his eyes into the food making it salty. Putting his plate aside, Govind's thoughts raced back to 6 years…..

"Why can't I go out ma?" Govind asked his mother who was taking care of his younger sister, Gopi. "I told you dear, it's not safe for you. Riots are taking place outside." His mother replied, a bit annoyed because he was asking the same question for the fourth time. Govind was of ten years then.

His mother was worried about his father who had gone to support the movement. "Why riots ma? Isn't the quit India movement supposed to be peaceful?" Govind asked innocently. His mother replied "yes it was supposed to be peaceful but the government isn't handling the protesters in a nice way."

Govind leaned against the wall quietly. Suddenly he heard a sound pitter-patter. It was raining! He looked outside the window. It was raining wildly! The sound of the raindrops falling on the ground had dominated the loud shouts of the Angry protests. His father had been out for quite a long time. Govind waited for him.

After few minutes he saw a small, shadow from far. 'Must be father!', a happy thought ran in his mind. The figure grew bigger and bigger and…. Alas! It was not his father. It was his father's revolutionary friend Ajmer Singh whom Govind called Kaka fondly. 'But why is he running towards our house?', came a question in his little mind.

He tried to go towards the entrance but his mother sent him inside and asked him to close the door. From inside, Govind could slightly hear the conversation going on and he looked outside through a small hole in the wooden door. Ajmer kaka was drenched all over and he was saying something. His face wore a sad expression.

Govind could only hear the words- riots….stick….. forehead…… Hospital. Kaka broke down into tears as he stopped. There was a sound as if someone had fell down. Govind tried to look at his mother but the small hole was not allowing him to do so. He slowly opened the door and walked out. His mother was sitting on her knees with her eyes full of tears. "Has something bad happened maa?"

Govind asked. Upon seeing Govind, his mother hugged him tightly without saying anything. Govind was perplexed. He could not understand the things happening around him. His mother's tears made his cheeks wet. Her sobbing did not stop.

A few people had gathered outside the house. Then a white mattress was bought on which a body was laying. It was of…… his father! Govind could not believe his eyes. His father's body was covered with a white sheet up to his shoulders and his nostrils were filled with cotton buds. His father was……. dead! But how? His face became red, swollen and violent drops of water started flowing from his eyes.

His mother ran and sat beside her husband's lifeless body. That day she cried and cried till no tears were left in her eyes. Even little Gopi seem to be mourning through her continuous shrill baby cries. Everything went black before Govind's eyes.

After weeks of his father's last rites, Govind was preparing a hot cup of tea for his mother. She had been ill since his father's demise. Her fever was rising day by day despite of taking medicine regularly. It was up to Govind to take care of her and his sister…. and on one fateful night, his mother breathed her last.

Unfortunately, without her mother's milk, little Gopi could not survive for long. Govind's whole world shattered before him. He was left with nothing. It was too much for a ten year old.

But the series of mishaps didn't end. His house was seized by the government in the name of penalty. Since then a homeless Govind had been working in small daily based jobs for survival.

That was the day he realised that nothing comes free of cost, not even freedom. Everything has a cost and the cost for freedom was sacrifice. Sacrifice of Life, happiness, harmony and everything……

END

The Massacre

"Where is the newspaper, Shanti?" came a loud booming voice which woke up Sohan from his sleep. It was his father's voice. The first thing he wanted every morning was the newspaper with a hot cup of tea. Sohan quickly went to bath for he knew that his father liked young boys to be awake and ready early. Although Sohan was just 10 years old he always tried to match his father's expectations.

He walked out of the room and saw his father reading the newspaper while sitting on the rocking chair with a grim expression on his face. His mother entered the living room with a hot cup of tea in her hand. Upon seeing father's face she quickly asked "what happened? Has another person died? Has the government hanged anyone else?" Before his father could answer any of these questions, Sohan joined the conversation. "Yes baba, what is the cause of your tension?" His father looked at him surprisingly. "Are you sure you will be able to understand what I say." "Maybe or.... maybe not, but I will try to…" he answered. Amused by Sohan's words his father said, "OK, listen" then suddenly his voice turned grim. "The government has arrested doctor Saifuddin Kitchlew, Dr Satyapal and taken them to the secret location." "But why?" Sohan asked curiously to which his father replied, "because they actively participated in the satyagraha led by Gandhiji."

Sohan's eyes lit up on listening Gandhiji's name. Since he was 7 years old, Sohan had often heard about Gandhiji's name from his parents, teachers, newspapers and wished to meet him in person. Suddenly they were disturbed by the cries of his little brother, Amar. Mother went to check on him. Sohan once again turned his attention towards his father and asked, "how will the people respond to this Baba?" His father remained silent.

That night was a restless one for Sohan. His innocent little mind could not understand that how can someone be treated so unjustly. Next morning, he woke up to a sound. No, it was not his father's voice asking for newspaper or tea. It was more of a Stamping sound. As if a large number of people were walking together. Sohan quickly glance outside the window.

The city of Amritsar was in a furry. People from different parts of Punjab were marching together. Sohan quickly ran out of his room to the living room. "What happened?" he quickly asked, trying to catch his breath. His father was gazing out of the window.

"A large demonstration is assembling in the Jallianwala Bagh to protest against the arrest of Dr Kitchlew and Dr Satyapal", he replied. "And.......what about us?" Sohan asked. "Not you, only I am going. It's not safe for you", father replied. Just then his wife, Shanti joined the conversation "No, we will also come. It's for our nation and we are not the only women and children going", she said while pointing outside where large number of people including men, women and even small children were marching together. His father gave in "Fine!" He was proud of his family.

The four set out towards the Jallianwala Bagh along with the other people. None of the people were armed. His mother was carrying little Amar in her arms. Everyone had a stern look on their face and were determined to protest against the injustice done by the government. However..... none of them knew that this small movement was going to be of great significance in the history of Indian Nationalist Movement.

On his way Sohan saw many waving crop fields ready to be harvested and he remembered that it was the festival Baisakhi!

Sohan noticed that the Bagh had ten feet tall walls surrounding it from all four sides. There was only one gateway to the Bagh which served both the purposes of entrance and exit.

"I Wonder what would happen at the time of an emergency" came thought in his mind. It seemed that along with the protest for the deportation of the two leaders people had also gathered to celebrate Baisakhi. Everyone greeted and wished each other with sweets and flowers.

Then begin the Peaceful protest. "Didn't the government ban gatherings having more than four people?" came a voice from within large crowd present there. "We are not armed, it's just a peaceful meeting. I don't think that the government will take action against us", said a man standing at the front. Another voice joined in "even if they object, we won't budge until our demands are fulfilled." The conversation continued

"They have to release doctor Kitchlew and doctor Satyapal...."

"It is our country and they have no right to arrest our leaders...."

"The government has shown great injustice...."

Sohan could not help but think that why even was India ruled by someone else. He had often read stories about ancient India, stories about Raja, Rani and their Kingdom. In these stories Marathas were ruled by a Maratha, Punjabis ruled by Punjabi and Indians and was ruled by an Indian. When did foreigners become a part of this?

Sohan looked around himself. The discussion was over and people were sitting silently but all of their faces said something. They were determined to compel the government to fulfill the demands. Even the children present there did not make any noise.

The Silence almost became awkward when suddenly there came a loud, rapid sound from the entrance of the Bagh. Everyone was startled and looked towards the sound's origin. Standing there were at least 10 British soldiers holding guns in their hands.

A person standing in the front went forward, "you cannot scare away with a single gunshot...." Boom! The bullet did not let him complete his sentence. It went inside his chest oozing out blood from his body. A sharp cry ran through his body, after which he fell down to the ground. Despite of all his efforts to stay alive the second bullet from the soldier's gun took his soul. It was the first time Sohan had witnessed death so closely. It was too much for a ten year old. But fate had much more of it stored for the young boy.

In no time a large number of soldiers started covering all sides of the bagh, including the only exit ready to kill any person in reach of their gunshot. All the protesters panicked. Sohan's mother pulled him closer and held Amar strongly. Those people who tried to go forward and negotiate were the first victims of the bullets. No one could get outside. The only option was to either run huffle-puffle or jump of the wall, both ways leading to death. Bullets were shot in all directions either wounding or killing innocent people protesting for their rights.

Sohan's family tried to stay together with his father shielding them. "Stay down... don't panic... nothing will happen... we will..." were his last words because just then he was shot by a fast bullet which entered his chest. Sohan was just behind him and was fully frightened "Baba!" a shrill and loud cry rose from his mouth. His father looked at him in horror as he fell. Tears sprang from Sohan's eyes. His mother was heartbroken. She wanted to sit beside her husband and mourn his death but, she didn't have the time. She had to save her kids life. She dragged Sohan and tried to find a safe place which was however impossible in a closed garden with only one exit surrounded by armed soldiers from all the sides.

The gunshots were not stopping. It seemed as the bullets had decided to take the life of each and every person present there. Sohan's mother, holding Amar in one hand, was exhausted. Then suddenly a random bullet chose her shoulder as the target and dug deep into it. A loud cry came from her mouth and she fell to the ground. "Maa!" he cried while taking Amar from her hands. "You must keep going", his mother said with tearful eyes. Even though the bullet hadn't hurt any of her vital parts she couldn't continue. She was completely worn out. She put her hands on Sohan's cheeks, wiped his tears and then..... she slept.

Sohan grabbed Amar with his blood covered hands trying to recover from what just happened. He wanted to save Amar and did not want him to meet the same fate as his parents. He saw the exit which was guarded by an armed soldier. He waited for him to get distracted, and just when that happened, he ran towards the exit. Even though most people inside had lost the hope of survival, Sohan still had the hope and the will to survive.

But alas! before he could reach the gate to survival, a bullet aimed at him went deep into his back which was fired so fast that it may have damaged his spinal cord. Although he had prevented Amar from getting hurt Sohan didn't know what would happen to Amar that. Sohan was badly hurt from the bullet. His whole back including his shoulders were aching. He felt dizzy and met the ground, still holding Amar in his hands....

....and as little Amar cried, Sohan closed his eyes and fell into a long slumber, to arise in his next birth hopefully free from foreign rule, bloodshed, and injustice.....

END

The Charge On The Crowd

---ꙮ---

There was a lot of Hustle and bustle going on in the streets of Darsana. Amidst this large crowd was Raghav - anxious, lost and crying. He was trying to find someone precious, his parents...

It all started in the morning. Raghav woke up and watched the outside proceedings with curiosity. Gandhiji had called the civil disobedience movement, asking the people to disobey the government, disown foreign goods. Nobody had the right to rule them or sell them foreign goods. Raghav was impressed by how Bapu broke the salt law and made salt by walking from Sabarmati to Dandi. No one, even the British thought that Gandhiji would be successful in completing the task.

Like him Raghav's father was also a great follower of Gandhiji and the civil disobedience movement. His family had boycotted all the British goods and were living on the food items, dresses and other essentials that were made in India. They were participating in civil disobedience Satyagraha. Adorned in white plain clothes, the family set out for the Satyagraha to contribute to the country's freedom movement. Although Raghav was just eleven years, he wanted to be a part of the civil disobedience movement. His family boycotted all foreign goods and set them fire.

They were from an upper middle class family and Raghav's father had a good reputation in his locality and neighbourhood. He helped people and led many demonstrations against oppressive British policies in a peaceful way. His family walked along him. Although their means were peaceful the government used repressive policies to stop the protests.

While the protestors among which Raghav and his family was sitting and doing a 'Dharna', the British officials emerged from nowhere and started a attacking on the protestors. There was huffle and puffle everywhere. Raghav's mother held him close. His father was already wounded and was bleeding on his forehead. Raghav could not believe it. What started as a peaceful demonstration ended up as a violent 'Lathi charge' against the protestors.

Then suddenly an official came behind his mother, ready to hit her with his lathi, but before he could do it Raghav's father looked behind and took the Lathi charge on his shoulder. "Run!" he cried. Raghav's mother reluctantly nodded and ran, taking Raghav by her hands. Raghav kept looking at his back to check whether his father was behind them or not.

Just when he thought anything worse couldn't happen he heard a sharp and loud sound of a bullet. The firing has started! "Ma! firing... the bullets", Raghav cried panicking.

His mother tried to reassure him but suddenly a bullet whizzed past her, giving her a near to death experience which startled her and she let go of Raghav's hand for a moment. But it was too late to catch hold of him again because the panicking crowd forced Raghav to get away from his mother. "Raghav!" his mother cried. "Ma!" He cried in reply.

.... and there he was trying to stand stiff amidst the bustling crowd searching for his parents. "Ma! Baba!" he kept on shouting. He thought as if the rushing crowd would trample him under their feet.

While he was walking continuously with tears in his eyes he started noticing his surroundings. People were fear striken and running helter - skelter. There was a lot of bloodshed. When he walked through the dead bodies lying on the ground he realized the importance of independence, for many people have been giving immense sacrifice for it.

While he was thinking about all these, he suddenly felt a huge pain on his shoulders as if it has been hit with a tremendous force. He turned back and saw a British official with a stick, standing there. "Why did you....", his sentence remained incomplete as the official hit him again. "Aah!", Raghav cried. His shoulders started bleeding.

He tried to run but the officer hit him again at the knee causing Raghav to fall down. "Argh!" he grunted in pain. The rocks on the ground gave severe cuts on his knees. Then the officer hit him again on the back sending a wave through Raghav's body and causing some blood to ooze out from his mouth. "Aaah!" he screamed again but it had no effect on the officer and he mercilessly gave another blow on Raghav's back.

Raghav didn't even have the energy to scream now. His eyes became drowsy. The officer smiled, satisfied. He walked away, leaving the boy on his own.

"Why? Why me? What was my fault?", were the things going on in his mind...... but he was not the only one. Many children and women met the same fate that day. "Maa....Baba...." were the only words he kept on saying while lying there until he found them both........ in heaven.

END

Sacrifice, Pain And Love

"...... and once again wish you all a happy 53rd Independence day", said headmaster Shankar concluding his long speech. It was 15th August 2000. "Today on this special occasion, students of primary section will be taken to Red Fort for the field trip."

Two friends Sudha and Mihir, both in 5th standard, standing in the Assembly line had different views on the field trip. "Couldn't they have chosen a better place for field trip instead of the Red Fort", snorted Mihir.

"Oh, Mihir think about the fun, the things we will learn today. We may get to know about the stories related to it. How exciting!" exclaimed Sudha.

Mihir just gave a 'whatever' expression and started looking around the school. It was covered with tricolour banners, posters, balloons and even the teachers were dressed in tricolour clothes. Near the entrance a big Rangoli was made with the colours- orange, white and green. "Why was the school not decorated so grandly during Diwali or Christmas?" he thought aloud.

Suddenly a sharp and loud ringing sound ran through the Assembly hall. It was the bell ringing, signalling the end of the assembly and students to get ready for the trip. Students cheerfully entered the bus, happy to get rid of the classes at least for one day. All the other students chatted excitedly throughout the way but Mihir silently gazed outside the window looking the least interested.

Then Kirti mam cleared her throat, "listen students, as you all are visiting the famous monument Red Fort, you might as well know something about it." All the students look eagerly towards her except Mihir. "Do you know why it is called the Red Fort? ...because it's made up of red sandstone", she said, answering her own question.

"On 15 August 1947 the Indian flag was hoisted near the Red Fort for the first time after independence by Prime Minister Jawaharlal Nehru....and children, if any of you is Caught damaging the walls of the fort by writing or drawing something on it, then you will surely be punished", Kirti ma'am warned.

Soon they reached their destination. "Ok children you may roam around here but when I call you, everyone should assemble near the Gate", mam announced.

Mihir and Sudha went towards the Fort. "It's just like few red sand bricks standing on top of each other", remarked Mihir. "Seriously! It's a fort which almost

resembles a small Castle. There is so much to see here", cried Sudha. "Whatever, it is boring!" retorted Mihir.

Before Sudha could counter that remark, a voice came from behind her, "Boring is it?" The children turned around to see where the voice came from.

It was an old man in his sixties wearing a white kurta. He walked towards them. "Do you really think that this is just a pile of red bricks standing on top of each other?", He asked Mihir while pointing to the Red Fort spread over 255 acres of land with Islamic, Hindu and Persian architectural style.

Mihir looked again at the almost octagon Fort enclosed by long and strong walls. "Well... not really but surely a trip to the zoo or Garden would have been much Better", he replied vaguely. He did not like the way the old man interfered in their conversation.

Sudha was more polite. She introduced herself and asked, "what is your name Sir?" The old man smiled at her, "Myself Manoj Kumar." Then he turned to Mihir, "maybe listening to a small story will change your perception." Sudha eagerly looked on.

The old man started, "That day I woke up earlier than my usual time because I could hear something. Not someone's voice. It sounded like a procession going

on. I used to live in a Villa and my bed was located just next to the window. I looked down from it and to my astonishment lots of people from different places were parading towards the "Lal Kila." Amongst them were dancers and singers singing about India's Fame. I was just eleven years old and didn't know what was exactly happening still the procession excited me and I went to join it."

The old man was narrating the incident as if he were cherishing his old memories.

"There I saw that many people were wearing white and carrying the tricolour flag. The whole Delhi city was decorated with the colours Orange, white and green. There was a large gathering near the Red Fort. When I made my way through the crowd, imagine my surprise when I saw Jawaharlal Nehru addressing the crowd with a speech. I did not understand much but I was really fascinated. After his speech he hoisted our flag near this same Red Fort. This was followed by many performances of dancing and singing. I was very happy. All our pain, struggle, and sacrifice had finally bore fruit...." the old man ended.

By that time Mihir had gained a little interest, but he had one question, "You were just eleven years old. How could you feel the pain and sacrifice behind independence?"

The old man smiled sadly, "you don't know what I had gone through" he said, his voice cracking.

"My father used to serve in the army when I was small. In 1942, he joined the Azad Hind Fauj formed by Netaji Subhas Chandra Bose. They fiercely fought against the British to secure Independence but sadly, failed..... and in this my father lost his life.

I remember people bringing his body to us. It was covered with blood. He had a dangerous death. In spite of this, his face adorned a Peaceful smile. To this day I am very proud of him", the old man said, trying to control his tears.

"I was in trauma for a few days after that," he continued, " My mother's state was the same but she also felt proud of father. And then in the month August, she participated in the Quit India Movement. She didn't want my father's sacrifice to be wasted. Unfortunately, my mother was badly wounded in the lathi charge. She succumbed to her injuries and died in September.

I was just eight and both my parents had left me. I was shattered completely.

Then I was taken to my guardian, my uncle. I spent rest of my childhood in my uncle's house. There I was an unloved child often alone and isolated. My uncle showered all his love upon my cousins where as his harsh words were reserved for me.

At the age of 10, I even thought of ending my life but then remembered my mother's last words, "Manu sorry for all this.... but you will have to live, even if life becomes difficult.... to witness the freedom of the country for which we have sacrificed our life", the old man said almost sobbing.

"So, you see.... I exactly know how it feels when we sacrifice something for the Country", the old man concluded. His eyes were wet and red. Sudha and Mihir did not know what to do. They could never imagine the pain in the old man voice, still they felt extremely sorry for him. They knew that nothing could replace his sacrifice. They tried to comfort him and gave him water.

Just then their teacher called them for departure. Mihir and Sudha walked away slowly as the old man shed tears in the memory of his late parents. Sudha and Mihir had learnt an important thing that day.

The Nationalist movement was beyond the writing of books and fort structures.

It was about the story behind it,

it was about the sacrifice made by numerous people,

it was about the pain they had to bear.....

it was about the love they had for their country.

END

The Terrors Of Partition

PART 1

It was very dark, though a small beam of light entered through an opening. On the other side of the opening was a tall man pointing a gun towards his father. His eyes were drowsy, his hands were on his laps. He was looking completely exhausted, fighting to stay alive. The tall man ignoring his pitiful condition, pulled the trigger of the gun and shot him. A loud crack!

Altaf instantly woke from his sleep, profusely sweating and breathing heavily. He quickly wiped his face and looked around himself. It was just a dream, a dream that he gets often. Altaf quickly went and washed his face. Then he looked at the photo of his family. His eyes became moist. His parents were no more with him. They had died during a time when India although independent, was stained by communal riots.....

Altaf belonged to a small district in Punjab. On 15th august, they were elated when India was announced independent, but before the freedom from colonial powers was celebrated nicely, the stench of religious differences, communal riots and hindu – muslim fights had started spreading all over India, especially Punjab.

21ˢᵗ September 1947

9 year old Altaf was eating his dinner with his father when someone started knocking on their door furiously. His father opened the door and saw a huge man at their doorstep. It was their neighbour, Mohan. He barged into Altaf's house. Behind him were many others.

"What happened Mohan? you are here at this time!", Altaf's father asked, surprised. Mohan stopped him by lifting his hand. "You better leave this house. Actually, you better leave Punjab and travel to Pakistan, land for people like you," he spoke stiffly. Altaf and his family members were taken aback. "What!?", his father cried. "You do not belong here now!" shouted Mohan and went outside slamming the door behind him.

Altaf innocently asked, "baba, all our neighbours were so friendly with us, how did such a sudden change occur in their behaviour?". His father sighed, "differences have become far more powerful than long years of friendship dear". Altaf's parents were prepared for this. They started packing important things in cloth and tied them in bundles. They had to leave soon as the situation outside was becoming tense.

"Maybe our neighbour was right, we do not belong here now. It's not safe here for us anymore," Altaf's mother said, sadly. "At any moment they can barge into our house and....", a tear fell from her eye. Altaf's father assured her, "we will stay together and will safely reach Pakistan". "But I want to stay here baba! How can we leave our homeland?" Altaf asked. His father did not say anything but he was sad.

Soon he hanged the bundle of important items on his shoulder and mother held Altaf firmly. They were on their way to get a train, The Amritsar train. The situation there was tense, people of religion were fighting with the others. Communal differences had killed humanity. However, Altaf's innocent mind interpretated it as a large number of people fighting together like animals.

The ground looked like a battle field with number of corpses. Many Hindus and Sikhs were migrating to east Punjab and the Muslims were migrating to west Punjab, to Pakisthan. The police and other servicemen instead of protecting the migrants were provoking the riots. There were gunshots from everywhere. Swords and spears were also used. Altaf and his family shielded themselves using lids of water containers and after much difficulty were able to board the train. Altaf was happy and his mother was relieved that they were safe but Altaf's father wasn't sure.

22nd September 1947

About 30 miles east from Amritsar there was a loud scream in the train. Altaf was terrified. His father, also shocked, looked from his seat. The train had stopped. About a dozen men boarded the train with swords and spears in their hands. They swept through the train, trying to kill, men, women and children. Altaf's father assured his family members, and sent them to the back of the train.

The attackers were successful in killing a few people but their assault was beaten off due to their small number. Altaf's father, though having a few cuts on his body, breathed a sigh of relief. However, destiny had much more for him to see. For the rest of the journey, Altaf sat very close to his mother as he was very much frightened by the recent violence. His father ran his fingers over his head to comfort him.

After sometime the train came to a halt. It had reached it's destination. The passengers were getting ready to get off the train when sudden shouts were heard from the front. "They are attacking us again!", cried someone.

A large number of armed men barged into the train. This time their assault couldn't be stopped, they were many. They had swords and sickles. People tried to save themselves by going back, but in vain as they couldn't stop the attackers due to their large numbers. Many hid their children in boxes, cloth bundles and blankets. Altaf's father searched for another exit to get out of the train safely. He made Altaf lay on a blanket, rolled it and carried it over his shoulders Altaf's mother walked closely behind him. They were at the back of the train and the bad men were advancing quickly, stabbing and severing all the people in their way. The cries of innocent children being separated from their parents and seeing them getting killed in front of their own eyes was unbearable.

Altaf's family came near to the exit. His parents quickly unrolled the blanket and let Altaf out who immediately hugged his mother. His mother comforted him and wiped his tears. As soon as they stepped out of the train, a bullet hit her forehead. Gunshots were being shot from both the sides to kill any person who might have escaped the slaughter inside the train. The assault was much bigger than one could think. "Ammi", a cry rose from Altaf's mouth. His mother fell to the ground and Altaf's father sat beside her, holding her hand. He knew she wouldn't survive. Her eyes closed and tears came from his.

He quickly regained his senses and carried Altaf, who had become unconscious in his arms. Before he could get to a safe place, a bullet hit him on his left leg and he stumbled. Looking behind, he saw two extremists, one with a sword and another with a gun. They both were advancing towards him. Altaf's father started walking as fast as he could with his limping leg. Luckily, he was shielded by a group of people rushing hurriedly in different directions. Thus, the men lost track of Altaf and his father.

The railway platform of Amritsar was looking like a battlefield. Altaf's father held him tightly to safeguard the him from the blows of swords given by huge men. At last, he saw a turning and breathed a sigh of relief. Quickly, he walked towards it and saw a bundle of hay where he placed Altaf.

"Baba, where are we? Where is mom?", asked Altaf weakly as he opened his eyes. "Altaf…. stay here till I call you", his father said and hid Altaf inside the bundle. Just as he was about to check for help, he felt a throbbing pain in his head. He screeched in agony and held his head. Turning back, he saw a muscular man with a gun, who had used the back of the gun to hit his head. A gunshot on his knee forced him down.

All this noise alarmed Altaf. He tried to look out through a small opening and saw his father sitting on the ground, dangerously wounded, being targeted with a gun by another huge man. The man pulled the trigger and the bullet went through his father's forehead.

Altaf wanted to cry out loud as his father fell to the ground, but he couldn't find his voice. He had witnessed both his parent's death that day. Tears ran from his eyes but he was too scared to get out.

Finally, he was rescued by some people and taken to a makeshift refugee camp in Pakistan. Many people died there but Altaf survived as he didn't have any fatal injuries. However, one thing which never left him was the trauma of loss and separation. He was adopted by some old couple in need of help in old age. The rest of his childhood passed of calmly but he always felt the absence of his parents.

Altaf was 25 now, and 16 years to that dreadful incident, he still couldn't forget the terrors of partition……

END

The Terrors Of Partition

PART 2

Ten year old Mandeep was listening to the radio along with his father, sitting in the living room. The situation was tense in the past few days. News was that, partition was going to be announced. Mandeep's father knew that partition wouldn't be an easy and simple journey from west Punjab to East Punjab, it would include massive crowds, riots and bloodshed. These had started even before the official announcement of partition. He looked towards Mandeep's innocent eyes which had a mixture of fear and curiosity in them who asked, "what should we do now baba?"

Mandeep's father did not want Mandeep's childhood to be influenced by communal intolerance and bloodshed, but he had no choice. "We will have to get out of here fast", said Mandeep's Mother. The family lived in Khewra. There had been attacks in Khewra By religious extremists who burnt a large number of houses. All the Hindus were asked To evacuate as soon as possible. Mandeep and his family had already packed their important belongings and were prepared to leave.

25th September 1947

As the family left for the railway station, they saw a large number of people collected there. Mandeep asked his mother- *Ma what will happen if the Muslims attack us during our journey?* His mother replied- *no dear they will not. Even if they attack us, all of us are armed and will be able to defend ourselves.* Since Independence there had been many incidents of Refugee train massacres and so everyone wanted to be prepared for anything that can happen during the journey.

All the passengers boarded the train at Pind Dadan Khan. The passengers were told that the train would go to Ferozepur. People inside the train were silent and just prayed that they reach their destination safely. Mandeep noticed that along with the passengers, there were 15 men from the Pakistani military present in the train. After sometime Mandeep started feeling hungry. His father assured him that once the train stops, he would buy Some food from the provisional Store.

At night the train came to a halt at Kamoke station and all the passengers were informed that the train would stay there for the whole night. Mandeep's father tried to purchase some food from the Provision Store but was stopped from doing so. No one else dared to get out of the train as they were afraid of unexpected attacks. Poor Mandeep had to make do with water for that night.

No one was able to sleep peacefully as they were afraid and uncertain about waiting in Kamoke for one whole night. Past midnight a shrill voice was heard. It was the cry of a baby. The mother was trying hard to console her.

A Pakistani military person, angry for being disturbed from his sleep walk towards the mother and the child. "Hey you, put the child quickly to sleep or else...", He shouted and the child became frightened and started crying more loudly. The infuriated man started shouting and hurling insults on the woman. He was about to hit her when he was stopped by a hand.

It was Mandeep's father. "Can't you see that the lady is trying to calm the child", Mandeep's father said. The man pushed Mandeeps's father and said, "Mind your own business", then he turned towards the woman, "Shut the baby's mouth quickly!". Mandeep ran towards his father, "baba, are you fine". His father nodded. Mandeep's mother helped the woman to put the child to sleep.

26th September 1947

At about 8 am the next morning, when the train was about to leave, the police force ordered all the passengers to get down the train as they had to search the train. The passengers reluctantly did as asked. Each and every article of the passengers, males and females were checked. The police also ordered the passengers to give all their weapons, although most of the guns and riffles were licenced. The passengers hesitated but gave their weapons as they were said that, until the search is over, the train would not move from there.

Mandeep's mother was worried, "if we give away our weapons, then how will we able to defend ourselves in case of an attack?" her husband replied, "you are right, I feel suspicious. Nobody attacked us till now because we were armed, but now we are not". The police promised to return the weapons as soon as the search is over. The passengers anxiously waited for the search to get over for 2 hours.

Mandeep was also tensed seeing the worried faces of his parents. After the search was over the police, without giving back the weapons, asked the passengers to get into the train with their luggage so that the journey could resume. When everyone was inside a whistle came indicating that the train is about to start. The passengers were relieved as now they were going to reach Firozepur safely.

However just then, there came a high pitched shout, "Ya Ali!"

A huge crowd emerged from the market. All the men were armed! Armed with Rifles, Churas, axes, and other lethal weapons. As they came near the train, the passengers panicked as they did not have their arms and without them it would be difficult to defend themselves. The crowd barged inside the compartments and started butchering the passengers. However, they were only attacking the male passengers.

Mandeep's parents pulled him close. He was very scared but then noticed the police and his heart filled with hope. "They will save us now", he thought. However, to his extreme surprise the Inspector picked his gun, pointed it towards a passenger and shot him. Soon all the police force joined the crowd in killing the passengers. The 15 men from Pakistan military lifted their guns and started firing towards the sky.

Everyone was confused and after a few seconds, the military men joined the massacre and started shooting. Mandeep's father spotted the exit and tried to run away with family, but alas! Before they could reach the exit, one of the attackers gave a serious wound on his arm with his sword. Mandeep gave a terrified cry and ran towards his father who was hit by another bullet on the shoulder. The police and military were ready with their guns to shoot anyone who tried to escape. His father fell down and Mandeep's mother, overcome by grief, sat near him weeping.

Just Then Mandeep saw an armed man nearing towards them. "Ma! he is coming towards us. ma!" Mandeep cried, half weeping and half frightened. It was too late, the person grabbed his mother's hand and started dragging her. Mandeep held to her hand and they both were taken to one corner of the train where the rest of the women and children were there. Mandeep thought that the attackers were going to spare the women and children but one look at the mob's angry face clearly told him that he was wrong. Mandeep could do nothing other than hold back his tears as his mother's chain, bangles and earrings were forcefully removed. Suddenly his eyes caught an old woman begging the others for some water as her throat was parched. She reminded him of his late grandmother.

He remembered that he had some water left with him and went towards the old lady to help her. However, he was pushed aside by a mob and then to his utter shock, the mob held the old woman by her hair and flung her to the ground. Mandeep squeezed his eyes shut as the mob severed the old woman's head. All the elder ladies met with the same fate. Still, he felt safe beside his mother. Even though her valuables were taken, no one attacked her and the other women of her age. Suddenly a hand grabbed his and started to pull him. Mandeep, caught in a frenzy of fear, hugged his mother. His mother also held him tightly. He saw the person who was pulling him. It was one of the 15 men of the military. Despite of his mother's protests, Mandeep was snatched away from her. His face became red and moist as he cried out in terror, "Maaa...!", Mandeep cried. His mother was held back by two mobs. She tried her best to move forward but could not over power them and could not stop her son from being dragged on the ground and thrown out of the compartment.

Mandeep was striked thrice with a huge stick and left howling with pain on the platform. His mother's voice quivered as she begged the mobs to let her go near him. Amidst this pandemonium he started feeling drowsy. He saw his mother getting dragged away. Mandeep did not know where she was being taken, whether she was being spared or was going to be given a fate worse than death. Mandeep wanted to protest but he had no strength. So instead, he closed his eyes.

END

The Harsh Truth

It was a bustling day at thane's Mazdoor Naka. Laborers and construction workers were getting ready for their tiresome day, while some others were trying to catch the attention of contractors, who could hire them for a day or so. Sumesh and Mani, two laborers in their forties, were sitting in a corner and drinking. Twenty five year old Sumeet approached them and asked – "kaka, drinking so early in the morning?"

"You won't understand", Mani replied, smiling weirdly.

"Try me"

"We won't be able to tolerate the day if not for this magic potion."

Sumeet gave a dubious expression and walked away. *Maybe their work was really tiresome or... maybe not. Drunkards can easily make excuses for drinking.* At about 8 o'clock, Mani and Sumesh slowly got up and started walking towards the railway station. By that time few trains had arrived and the passengers started descending rapidly. All the workers assembled. Their employer shouted, "quick! Get to your work." The workers obliged and started picking something from the tracks with their bare hands. If seen from the back, it looked like a person was looking for something that had fallen on the tracks.

While the laborers were toiling near the station, Sumeet was sitting in an interview for local school teacher's job. "Hmm, your qualification is just enough for this job but there is a small problem. We have two other candidates waiting outside who are Brahmin and you are-"

"Please don't use that word sir", Sumeet interrupted quickly.

"....of lower caste", said the principle after a pause.

"This is wrong sir. You can't refuse me the job on the basis of my caste. The government has banned such practices", protested Sumeet. The principle smiled slyly and leaned closer, "Now, I don't believe than an officer will come and make rounds of the school if you go and complaint once."

Sumeet wanted to say something but knew that his words will go waste. He quickly got up and walked out before further humiliation. He was depressed, his glasses became foggy. "Where should people like us go? With the limited education we have, there are already less opportunities. This discrimination makes the situation even worse." With all these thoughts running in his mind, he walked towards to station. He saw Sumeet and Mani and went to meet them.

However, a shocking sight awaited him. The workers were picking feces and other disgusting materials from the railway tracks. Sumeet was appalled. How could something like that be touched by bare hands? He was disgusted by just seeing them do the work. How could the workers deal with it without any mask or gloves?

"Kaka! Stop it, drop that thing. What are you doing?" Sumesh looked up. He replied calmly, "why are you shocked? This is our work, our livelihood."

"Work! You call this work? This is disgusting and humiliating", Sumeet further said.

The workers, unmoved, continued to do their work. Sumeet was baffled and went on with his words. "Why are you people still doing this, please stop!"

This time Mani spoke and the other workers also joined-

"What else should we do? Do you think we like doing this?"

"We are doing this because we are stuck with this. We have no other means of livelihood."

"Our caste does not allow us to find respectful jobs."

Sumeet could not understand why everyone was using their caste as a justification for their livelihood. He was of the same caste but never thought of doing such a humiliating work. "You all don't understand. The government has termed manual scavenging as illegal. If you are forced to do so, you can take aid from government", he explained.

As Sumeet looked earnestly, the workers didn't seem convinced. A number of thoughts ran through their mind-

Is it that easy?

What will we do after getting out of this job?

Will we be able to fill our stomachs?

Sumeet couldn't answer those questions or guarantee them security. He knew it was not easy... but he would not give up.

In vain did Sumeet go to the railway office and in vain did he explain the dangers of manual scavenging to the officers. He was pushed out of the office and told that one day, he too will have to give in to societal pressure and choose manual scavenging as his livelihood.

A month later Mani died of tuberculosis, his family perished. There was no one to take care of them. It seemed that everyone knew the cause but no one wanted to speak about it.

Sumeet was greatly disturbed by this. He became an activist and campaigned against manual scavenging. His efforts helped many to occupy a stable and respectful occupation. However, the shackles of manual scavenging and caste discrimination continue to bind many parts of our country.

END

The Father's Wish

1940

Madhav woke up from his sleep, ready for a new day. He quickly washed his face and headed off to work.

Madhav was a poor man and worked in a textile shop. His employer was a rich merchant, who lived in town, and seldom visited the shop. Most of the work was done by Madhav and the other workers. It was 8 in the morning. That day was not a busy one. Customers did not rush in as soon as he opened the shop. His first customer was a woman who wanted to buy a saree for her cousin's wedding. She seemed rich. While Madhav was entertaining her as she chose between the banarsi and baluchari one, he heard loud shouts from the other side of the shop. He quickly called Chotu to wait on the customer and rushed to see what caused the drama.

It was an *Angrezi* officer, who was screaming at a humbled Ramesh and using words which were unintelligible to Madhav. He was accompanied by two others wearing the same uniform. Madhav's employer had taught him to not provoke an officer and try to earn their goodwill for the shop. Madhav went up to the vexed customer and tried to calm him down. He asked Ramesh what the matter was. The Englishman wanted to return a garment that he had bought few weeks ago. The garment was torn and the officer wanted a refund. Ramesh had tried to make him understand that torn garments could not be returned but that only resulted in irritated yells from the other side.

Madhav thought better of that and offered a refund to the customer to prevent further nuisance. But lo! The Englishman's pride had been hurt. "First of all, your garment quality is low. Then you argue with me, a British officer, instead of doing the needful!", he said haughtily. Madhav was about to apologize when Ramesh suddenly said, "Sir, we have not done any mistake. As for our garments, they are the best in the whole area. It may have torn by excessive stretching... did you take the wrong size?" A lady watching the happenings from aside gave a little giggle. Madhav shot a horrified look towards Ramesh.

The white face of the *Angrezi* officer was now red with anger. He pulled Ramesh by his collar and muttered- *you rascal... how dare you!? You think I am wrong?* Ramesh fumbled for words to come up with an apology. Madhav tried to intervene but he was pushed aside. Then things started to become rough. The officer tried to prove his point and started tearing the clothes in the shop to shreds. the two men who accompanied him also joined in the ruffle. Madhav and Ramesh made a vain effort to save their shop as the officers were stronger. All the other customers were terrified and ran away.

Chotu entered the scene and saw Madhav being punched by one of the officers. Ramesh was laying on the ground. He tried to stop the officers but they continued to rip the garments and beat the workers. It was only when few locals interceded and separated the two parties that the brawl stopped. But a huge damage had already been done. The shop incurred loss due to the shredded garments and Ramesh and Madhav were badly hurt.

That night as Madhav sat in his hut and tended to his wounds, he recalled the events of the day. He thought that it was the power of the British over India that enabled the officers to do what they did that day. That event left a lingering wish in his mind. He wanted his children to live and breathe in a free India....

2010

Govind woke up to a new day, trying to forget the troubles of the previous one...

He rubbed his eyes and listlessly proceeded out of his house, which was made of mud bricks. There was a small bathroom outside, its entrance covered by a rickety door made of leftover construction materials. After completing his morning business, he walked towards the *maidaan*.

Govind was an orphan. His parents died early. They were poor and worked as laborers. Govind knew that his grandfather used to work in a textile shop but was fired due to some incident. Since then, the goddess of wealth never showed up at their home. Thus, Govind too became a laborer for survival.

On his way he met Sudhakar. 'Did you hear? The *sahib* has got new contracts. It seems we all have to work more in less wages for few days' he said. 'Really?' Govind was worried. It was already difficult for him to make ends meet. The overtime and reduced income would not help at all. He sighed. It was going to be a long day.

In the *maidaan*, the employer started hurling orders on the workers as they picked their tools and sacks. It was a construction site and indeed the sahib was more tense and strict that day. Govind and Sudhakar had to move bricks and sacks from one place to another without break. It was mid-summer and the sun was high up in the sky. The workers were struggling to keep their pace and do their tasks.

There was a soft thud heard..... it was Govind. He had fallen down under the weight of a huge sack. The others gathered around him. Soon the contractor saw the commotion and yelled 'What's all this nonsense? Get back to work everyone. We don't have a minute to spare.' He moved towards Govind and asked him to get up and pick the sack. Govind was too tired. He pleaded '*Sahib*, please let me sit for few minutes. I will soon get back to work.' The employer was unmoved. He kicked Govind and said spitefully 'You think I hired you to rest? Quit overacting and start your work. You wouldn't want your wages to be cut, do you?' He held the corner of Govind's shirt and forced him to stand. Then he let go and walked away with a warning look.

Struggling heavily, Govind was able to make it through the day. But his wages were cut. Perhaps it was the way of the *sahib* to tell that he won't tolerate any nonsense. That night he wondered if he could leave this harsh labour and do something better. But the lack of money forced him to lose hope. He was surely living in a free and independent India but the shackles of poverty and discrimination still seized him strongly. He was far from free.....

END

The New Girl

Unlike everyday, the classroom was not noisy with the shouts and gossips of students. It was unusually filled with faint whispers. There was a new girl in the class, but she was different. She was pale and thin, her hair was shabby, her clothes were scruffy and stitched at various places. All eyes stared as she entered the classroom, walked over to the last bench in the corner and sat there. The new girl shuffled uncomfortably in her seat as she tried to ignore the attention.

Aarna and Diya, two friends, were curious about the new girl. During lunch, they approached her to ask her name. "Rinki", she answered shyly. Suddenly Diya said in a loud voice, "Eww... what's that smell? Is it from your clothes? They look so old." Rinki was shocked. All the students in the class roared with laughter. Aarna glared at Diya who in response gave a shrug and walked back to her seat. Rinki could do nothing but lower her head and stifle a sob.

After a few days, everyone forgot about the new girl... no one cared to play with her, invite her for lunch or even talk to her. Rinki quietly sat in her corner, only speaking when asked to and otherwise living like an invisible person.

One day, she mustered some courage and went up to a group of girls chatting and eating together. She hesitated but asked, "Can I have lunch with you guys today?"

The girls looked dismissively towards Rinki.

"Go away! We don't talk to people like you."

"Yeah, you better find others like you or get used to having your lunch alone."

"Can't you dress better? You look so shabby!"

Rinki was dismayed- why are you people so rude!? Just because I am poor doesn't mean you can treat me so bad….

Well, this was what she wanted to say but couldn't. Instead, she choked up her tears and slowly walked off to a lonely corner.

Aarna witnessed this from a distance. She was sad and she even thought of helping Rinki, but she couldn't. She imagined herself as the new target of her classmates, being mocked for being friends with the new girl. So, she decided not to poke her nose in the matter. But then, how long could she ignore the pitiful state of the new girl…

A few days later, Rinki was cornered by a few boys. They snatched her bag and started bullying her.

"What was your name again? Rinki? Such a funny one…"

"You never speak in the class. Is it because your voice is croaky?"

"Where do you live? In the slums?"

"Did you ever see yourself in the mirror? You are so ugly."

The boys through her bag behind the school and left her alone. Rinki quickly started searching her backpack, all her books were in there. She had to climb the wooden fence which caused her shirt to tear off at the end.

As she was ruffling through the garbage and leaves to find her bag, someone called her from behind. It was Aarna. She had seen the boys bullying Rinki. She asked Rinki whether she was okay. There was no reply. Aarna sighed sadly but helped Rinki find her bag. When the bag was found, Rinki turned towards Aarna and softly uttered a thankyou. Then she quickly rushed towards her home.

The next day Aarna entered the class and went to the seat next to Diya, as usual. But something kept her from sitting there. Her best friend shot a questioning look at her. Aarna ignored that and walked back to the last bench. First Diya, then the other girls and then the whole class stared at Aarna as she asked Rinki if she could sit with her. Rinki was surprised but responded with a nod. Aarna smiled and sat down. Although it was awkward with everyone whispering about them, the two of them were soon engaged in a conversation. Aarna had made a new friend and she felt unusually happy.

END

The Contradiction

It was 6 in the morning. The streets of Sirsa weren't yet busy, but one big *haveli* in the middle of the street was already filled with the sweet and pious sound of prayers and recitations being sung to goddess Laxmi. The house belonged to a rich upper caste Hindu Brahmin, Trivedi Shastri.

After completing all his morning rituals, he sat down to read the newspaper and enjoy it with a cup of tea. The newspaper had the usual headlines, about the huge massacre in Punjab, about children being taken away, women being raped and men being slaughtered on both sides of the borders. This indeed saddened Trivedi but he was not scared. He was in a place where he was supposed to be – a Hindu in the newly bordered India.

He then set out towards the temple to do his daily job, becoming a medium between people and their god. On one side, he was given greetings by every person who passed, which he accepted with great pleasure and pride, for he was an upper caste Brahmin. While on the other side he saw the ruins of mosques and houses where Muslims had lived. He was remembered of his childhood friend Abdul....

"Vedi! You can't catch me!", eight year old Abdul cried as he ran over the hill. Trivedi, who was seven then, ran after him, puffing. This game of catch continued for a while until both the boys became tired and sat under a tree. They plucked few berries from the nearby bushes and started devouring them. "My father says that times are changing. He keeps saying that religions are becoming reasons for fights...." Trivedi said innocently.

"Even I've heard my parents talking about it. I really don't understand it."

"Me neither. I don't understand most of the things adults talk of."

"Anyway, why should we bother about that? Let's leave such topics to our fathers."

"Yeah, its your turn to catch me now....", saying this Trivedi ran off.

The pleasant memory gave way to the present situation as Trivedi reached the temple. He found a queue of people waiting to list out their grievances to the almighty. Trivedi quickly went inside and started the aarti while reciting prayers. Midway, the aarti was disrupted by a loud shriek. The temple bells were stopped. Everyone including Trivedi ran towards the entrance of the temple.

There they saw a moaning man forced to the ground, being beaten with sticks by two other men.

Trivedi came forward, "wait! What happened? Why are you beating this man?". Someone from the crowd replied, "This man isn't as innocent as he looks Pandit ji. He is a shudra!".

".....and he dared to enter the temple", added the other man furiously. The man categorized as a Shudra started weeping. "Please have mercy on me. I came here to pray for my wife who has been ill for the past few weeks. No doctor is willing to treat her. I have a small daughter waiting for me at home".

Few of the people in the crowd assembled started shouting,

"Don't make such excuses for trying to destroy the auspiciousness of this temple".

"What should we do if your wife is ill. It gives you no right to demolish our religion".

"You are a Shudra. How dare you enter the temple! You must be punished!".

Few people forcefully lifted the weeping Shudra and said intimidatingly, "Come! A punishment in the court awaits you!". The poor man cried, "no! please, if something happens to me who will take care of my ill wife and daughter? Please, please leave me!".

Trivedi was moved by the plight of this poor Shudra. He tried to go forward and console the man, but the eyes of all the people standing there, pointing accusingly towards the same man stopped him. If he were to go there and support or touch the Shudra, wouldn't he be named an outcaste.

He could just helplessly see the poor man identified as a lower caste being dragged away, moaning and weeping.

At that night there were many thoughts going on in Trivedi's mind.

The first - many great men have said that we should be the change we want to see in our society..... but is it that easy? If change was to start from you, won't the society exclude you?

However, he knew that it was just an excuse. He could have saved the man but his position and pride had gotten in the way.

He could blame that India is not really independent. It was still in the clutches of discrimination, communal intolerance and suffering. But India is just a name, a piece of land. What makes it a country, a feeling, is it's citizens.

We just have two options. To blame others for weakening our country or do something to strengthen it.

END

www.ingramcontent.com/pod-product-compliance
Lightning Source LLC
LaVergne TN
LVHW061622070526
838199LV00078B/7389